Louisburg Library
Library District No. 1, Miami County
206 S. Broadway, Louisburg, KS 66053
913-837-2217
www.louisburglibrary.org

BLAZERS

Spooked

GHOSTS OF THE RICH AND FAMOUS

BY EMILY RAIJ

Reading Consultant:

Barbara J. Fox
Professor Emerita
North Carolina State University

CAPSTONE PRESS
a capstone imprint

Blazers Books are published by Capstone Press,
1710 Roe Crest Drive, North Mankato, Minnesota 56003
www.capstonepub.com

Library of Congress Cataloging-in-Publication Data
Raij, Emily, author.
 Ghosts of the rich and famous / by Emily Raij.
    pages cm. — (Blazers books. Spooked!)
 Summary: "Describes reports of ghostly encounters with some of the world's deceased celebrities and entertainers"— Provided by publisher.
 Audience: Ages 8-14
 Audience: Grades 4 to 6
 ISBN 978-1-4914-4079-7 (library binding)
 ISBN 978-1-4914-4113-8 (ebook pdf)
 1. Ghosts—Juvenile literature. 2. Celebrities—Death—Juvenile literature. I. Title.
 BF1461.R34 2016
 133.1—dc23
                                            2015001330

Editorial Credits
Anna Butzer, editor; Kyle Grenz, designer; Morgan Walters, media researcher; Kathy McColley, production specialist

Photo Credits
Alamy: GL Archive, 14, 15; Corbis: Bettmann, 6, 7, Leemage, 11, John Springer Collection, 16, 17, Underwood & Underwood, (al capone mugshot) top right 9; Getty Images: Brian Hamill, 21, SuperStock, (edgar allan poe) top right 13; Glow Images: Michael Grecco, 24, 25, Superstock, 23; iStockphoto: drnadig, 12, 13; Library of Congress: (abe lincoln) bottom left 6, Lasky Corporation, cover; Newscom: akg-images, 19, JT Vintage/ZUMA Press, 27, Olivier Douliery/MCT, 28, 29; Shutterstock: CAN BALCIOGLU, 8, 9, D_D, (vintage photo frams and paper) throughout, D_D, (paper notes) throughout, Fer Gregory, cover, Konstantin Sutyagin, (red curtain) 1, 22, Maksim Shmeljov, 4, 5, Phase4Studios, (spotlight background) 2, 3, 30, 31, 32, Sergey Peterman, cover, Sociologas, (old paper strip) throughout, STANZI, (castle) bottom right 14, Tueris, (grunge texture) throughout

Printed in China by Nordica
0415/CA21500562
032015   008844NORDF15

TABLE OF CONTENTS

SPIRITS OF THE STARS

Criminals, movie stars, musicians, and a magician! It's not a Halloween costume party. But the stories of these famous ghosts are just as entertaining! Do people really see the **spirits** of these stars?

spirit—the soul or invisible part of a person that is believed to control thoughts and feelings

ABRAHAM LINCOLN
(1809–1865)

Is the ghost of Abraham Lincoln wandering around the White House? Presidents, first ladies, and guests claim to have seen him. Sometimes Lincoln even appears in his old bedroom.

DID YOU KNOW?

Even some of the dogs that lived in the White House got spooked around Lincoln's bedroom. President Reagan's dog barked and growled outside the door. The dog refused to go in the room!

AL CAPONE (1899–1947)

Visitors to Alcatraz prison say banjo music comes from the cell of Al Capone. The **gangster** played the banjo in a prison band. The ghosts of other **criminals** may also haunt this abandoned California prison.

gangster—a member of a criminal gang

criminal—someone who commits a crime

DID YOU KNOW?

Some people believe Capone's ghost also haunts his gravesite in Illinois.

ANNE BOLEYN (1501–1536)

Anne Boleyn was the queen of England from 1533 to 1536. People believe she haunts many different places. Boleyn's ghost is often seen at the Tower of London. She was **executed** there by order of her own husband, King Henry VIII.

execute—to put to death

EDGAR ALLAN POE (1809–1849)

Does Edgar Allan Poe's ghost visit his gravesite on his birthday? The heartbroken author lost many loved ones before his death. He is buried in Baltimore, Maryland.

DID YOU KNOW?

Edgar Allan Poe wrote spooky stories and poems. One of his most famous poems is called "The Raven."

The Raven "Nevermore"

BURIAL PLACE OF

ALLAN POE

QUEEN ELIZABETH I (1533–1603)

Elizabeth was the queen of England, Ireland, and Wales from 1558 to 1603. Many royal family members believe they have been visited by the ghost of Queen Elizabeth I. She appears dressed in black and often haunts the Royal Library of Windsor Castle in England.

15

HARRY HOUDINI
(1874–1926)

Harry Houdini was one of the best escape artists and magicians of all time. But he didn't escape death in 1926. Some people say his ghost haunts the ruins of his California home. Could it be another one of Houdini's famous **illusions**?

illusion—something that appears to be real but isn't

DID YOU KNOW?

Mystery surrounds Houdini's death. Some say he was poisoned. Others say his appendix burst after he was punched in the stomach.

JESSE JAMES (1847–1882)

The events in Jesse James' life are as famous as the **legend** of his ghost. James led a gang of robbers in the Old West. He is said to haunt his family's old farm in Missouri. He may also haunt the St. James Hotel in Alabama where he often stayed.

DID YOU KNOW?

Jesse James was killed by a member of his own gang who shot him for **reward** money.

legend—a story handed down from earlier times; legends are often based on fact, but they are not entirely true

reward—something you get for doing something well

19

JOHN LENNON (1940–1980)

John Lennon was a member of the famous band The Beatles. The talented musician was gunned down by a fan in 1980. But his spirit may not rest in peace. Some people say Lennon haunts his old apartment building.

DID YOU KNOW?

Members of The Beatles said they felt Lennon's presence in the studio while recording an album together after his death.

MARILYN MONROE (1926-1962)

Hollywood starlet Marilyn Monroe died in her Los Angeles, California home. Some people say her ghost is still there. Others say she haunts the Hollywood Roosevelt Hotel. Guests have seen her ghost in a mirror and by the pool.

23

MICHAEL JACKSON (1958-2009)

The "King of Pop" wowed fans for **decades** with his singing, dancing, and flashy outfits. Sightings of his ghost began after his death in 2009. Fans say they saw Jackson's ghost at his memorial service in Los Angeles.

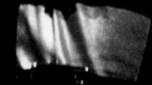

decade—10 years

RUDOLPH VALENTINO (1895–1926)

Rudolph Valentino starred in many silent films before his death. About 100,000 people lined New York City's streets for his funeral. Lots of fans means lots of ghost sightings! People claim to have seen his ghost in hotels, homes, and cemeteries.

DID YOU KNOW?

In 1930 a woman dressed in black and carrying red roses visited Valentino's **crypt** on the anniversary of his death. Since then, many of these women are seen there each year.

crypt—a room or building that holds a dead body

27

GONE BUT NOT FORGOTTEN

Nobody knows for sure if ghosts are real. But people often report sightings of celebrity ghosts. Are these famous spirits trying to tell us something? Or are fans just trying to hold on to their favorite stars?

GLOSSARY

criminal (KRI-muh-nuhl)—someone who commits a crime

crypt (KRIPT)—a room or building that holds a dead body

decade (DEK-aid)—10 years

execute (EK-si-kyoot)—to put to death as punishment for a crime

gangster (GANG-stur)—a member of a criminal gang

illusion (i-LOO-zhuhn)—something that appears to be real but isn't

legend (LEJ-uhnd)—a story handed down from earlier times; legends are often based on fact, but they are not entirely true

reward (ri-WAWRD)—something you get for doing something well

spirit (SPIHR-it)—the soul or invisible part of a person that is believed to control thoughts and feelings

READ MORE

Axelrod-Contrada, Joan. *The World's Most Famous Ghosts.* The Ghost Files. Mankato, Minn.: Capstone Press, 2012.

Frisch, Aaron. *Ghosts.* That's Spooky. Mankato, Minn.: The Creative Company, 2013.

Polydoros, Lori. *Top 10 Haunted Places.* Top 10 Unexplained. North Mankato, Minn.: Capstone Press, 2012.

INTERNET SITES

FactHound offers a safe, fun way to find Internet sites related to this book. All of the sites on FactHound have been researched by our staff.

Here's all you do:

Visit *www.facthound.com*

Type in this code: 9781491440797

INDEX